A New Planet to Call Home

Story by Carmel Reilly
Illustrations by Mariano Epelbaum

Contents

Chapter 1

Out of the Pod

It was dark when I opened my eyes. I had been dreaming I was on a spaceship, flying across the universe, and for a moment I didn't know if I was awake or asleep. I tried to call out for my guardian, Olag, but no sound came from my mouth. It wasn't until I heard the recorded message, "This sleep pod will open in ten seconds," that I remembered ...
I really was on a spaceship, flying across the universe.

The door to my sleep pod flew open and, thankfully, Olag was right there in front of me.

"You're awake, Okadi!" he said, hugging me and helping me out of the pod at the same time.

"Am I the last one to wake up?" I asked, looking around to see a crowd of people standing about.

"You are. But it's good timing," said Olag, pointing to the window. "Because we've just had our first glimpse of our new home planet, K22!"

I rubbed my head. It felt a little sore, but that's apparently what happens when you sleep for ten years. Everyone on our spaceship had been kept in a frozen state in our sleep pods while we travelled across the universe to our new home. This meant that when we woke up, we were all exactly the same age as when we left.

I gazed out the window at the planet below. It was strange how much K22 looked like our home planet Faya, which made me feel happy and sad all at once.

The reason we were in the spaceship was because Faya's sun was dying, which meant Faya was slowly burning up. When Fayan scientists realised this centuries ago, they began sending out robotic space probes to try to find another planet to live on. One of the probes finally came back with good news about a planet the scientists named K22.

Not only did K22 look like Faya, but apparently there were life forms there that were almost identical to us. The main differences were that those life forms had five fingers, while we had three, and they had fur on their heads, while we had none.

Like us, those life forms had taken over their planet. They had created cities and made vehicles that travelled on land, sea and air. However, compared to ours, their technology was old. K22 was similar to Faya many hundreds of years ago.

As I stared at K22, I could hear Olag and one of the engineers talking as they checked a map. The engineer said that usually we would circle the planet and scan it completely before landing. But because our spaceship had been damaged during the journey, we needed to get to the ground as quickly as possible.

"Are we going to land in the middle of a city?" Olag asked anxiously.

"Our scans show the city is empty," replied the engineer. "They also show that there is a large open area to land on and materials nearby that we can use for repairs. So, this seems like the best place for now."

Just then, the voice of the pilot came over the spaceship's communication speakers.

"Please strap yourself into a secure seat, ready for landing," she said.

Suddenly, I started to feel nervous. We were actually about to arrive at our new home. What would it be like down there on K22?

Chapter 2

Exploring K22

The atmosphere was thick with cloud and the ride was rough, but the pilot landed our spaceship with barely a bump.

When I looked out, I could see we were in the middle of a sandy open area. Dotted around us were what I thought must be dead trees. They looked similar to the ancient dead trees that could still be seen in some places on Faya. At the edges of the open area were lots of empty-looking, rundown buildings.

I turned to Olag. “What happened to this place? It looks so different from the images taken by the space probe.”

He shook his head. “The universe is so big. It took many years for our explorer space probes to return to Faya, and then many more for us to journey here ourselves. It seems that some disaster has occurred in the meantime.”

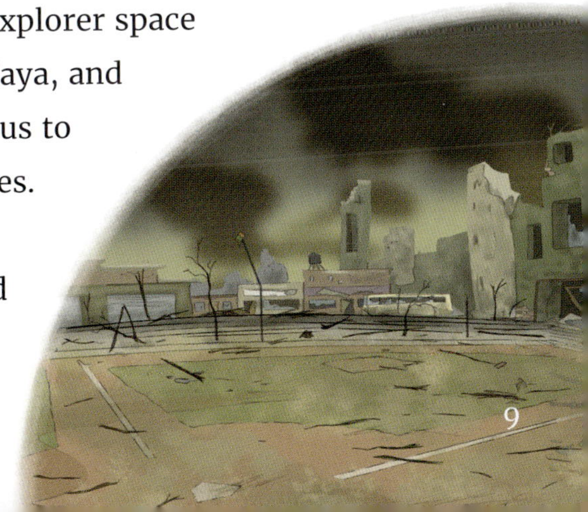

Just then, my friend Komot appeared beside me, grinning. “I think it looks interesting out there,” she said. “And I can’t wait to go exploring!”

“Well, you haven’t changed at all in ten years,” I said, giving her a big hug.

We had to wait while the engineers did some air testing to make sure it was safe for us to go outside. Once we were given clearance, Komot, her brother Humm and I went down to the storage area to retrieve some air-propelled hover-scooters. We used our hand prints to turn the scooters on, and in no time at all we were out riding around the surrounding streets.

It had been grey when we landed, but now the sun was coming out from behind the clouds and I began to notice signs of life. There were green shoots springing up from cracks in the road, and tiny furry creatures scuttled away as we passed by.

Finally, we stopped in front of a large building that looked different from the others. It seemed important in some way. There was some kind of writing or symbols on the front of it, but we had no idea what it meant.

"Apparently, the space probe didn't record the language of the local life forms," said Humm, sounding annoyed. "It would have been very useful."

"Shall we look inside?" I asked.

After checking over the building with his 3D scanner for anything dangerous, Humm declared the site was safe and we went in.

The place felt eerie. There were rows of shelves, some still holding objects that I had never seen before. Strangely, all these objects were similar. They looked like small folders with hard covers that held sheets of paper inside.

Paper was a product I recognised from visits to the museum on Faya. It was something that we used to write on centuries ago. But paper was very rare on Faya, and we stopped using it altogether when the heat killed the last of our trees.

I opened one of the folders and saw that the paper was covered with pictures and hundreds of lines of writing. I wondered what it meant. It looked nothing like Fayan writing.

After a few minutes, Humm said, "It's getting dark. We should get back to our ship."

I picked up a few folders with interesting pictures and threw them in my bag. I thought that it might be possible for the super-compu back on the ship to analyse the writing and translate it into Fayan.

Chapter 3

Who Is Out There?

I felt restless that night. I wondered how the others could sleep after snoozing for the past ten years. I filled the time in my cabin by looking at the strange folders and uploading them into my compu-wristband, which would automatically transfer them to the main super-compu later.

I had just finished doing this when I heard some faint noises. *Someone else must be awake*, I thought. Perhaps I could go and talk to them for a while?

I wandered around the corridors for a few minutes, but I didn't see anyone. It wasn't until I turned to go back to my cabin that I happened to glance out of a window and notice something. Was someone moving around out there? Whoever it was must have gone outside. I decided I would go out too, and say hello.

Luckily, I was close to the emergency slide, which is the quickest and most exciting way to get from inside the spaceship to the ground outside. The ship is as high as a six-storey building, which means normally we have to use the lifts or stairs to get down to the main entrance ramp. But it was the middle of the night, so who was going to tell me off for taking the easy way?

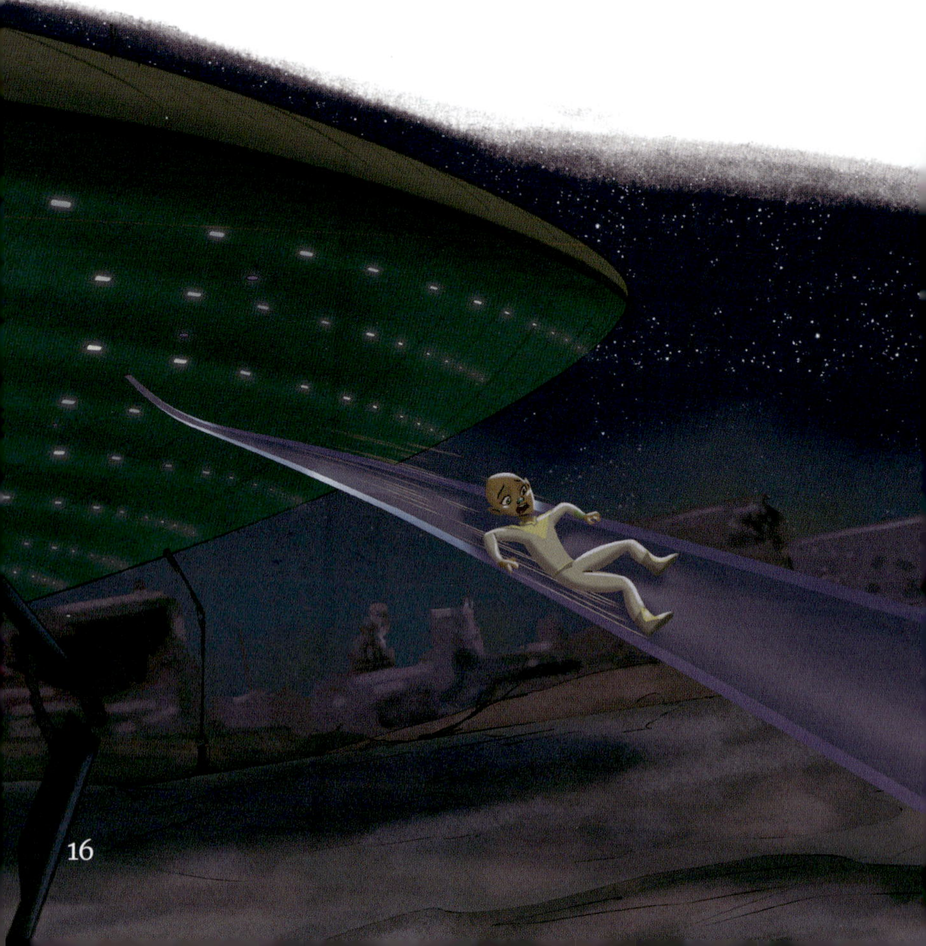

I opened the emergency door, edged onto the slide and pushed off. No sooner had I started whizzing downward than I realised I could hear voices. But these were not familiar voices. Not only were they speaking a language I didn't understand, but the words and the sounds they made were more like a strange, soft, jingling hum.

The engineers had said there were no life forms like us in this city. But somehow, I think they got that wrong. I felt fairly sure it wasn't Fayans I was about to meet down on the ground.

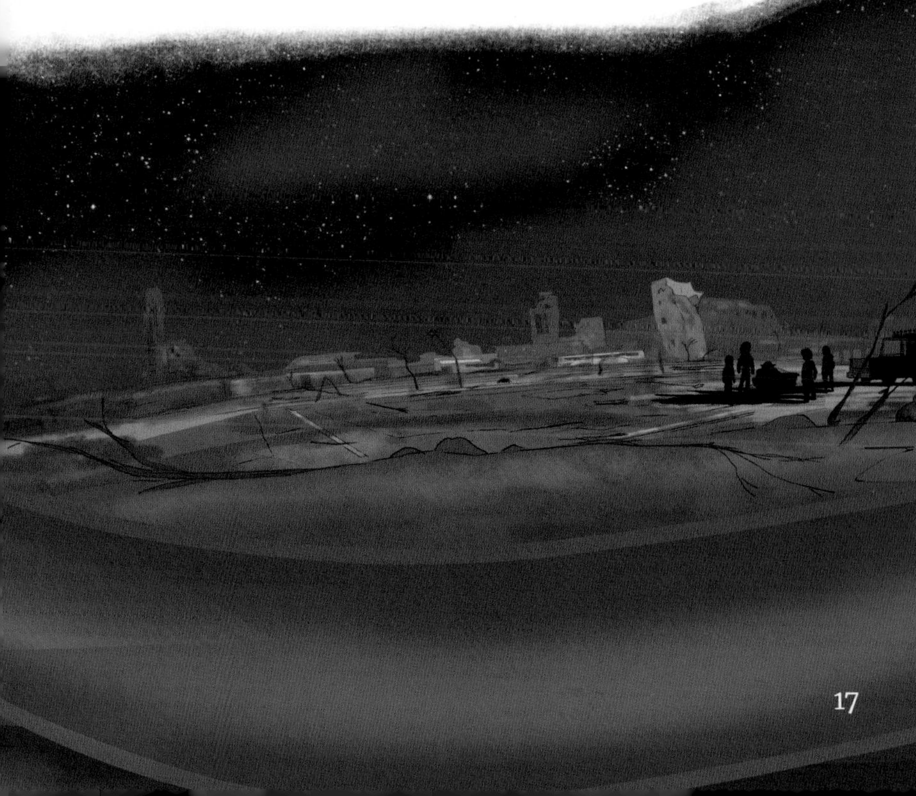

A jolt of fear hit me, and I desperately tried to stop myself from falling any further. But the slide was slippery, and clutching at the sides didn't slow me down. In seconds, I landed with a soft thud on the ground below.

Had whoever was down there heard me? It was quite dark and I couldn't see very far. I edged around the back of the slide and stood perfectly still, holding my breath. I couldn't hear voices, but after a while I realised I could hear other rustling and clinking sounds. I felt fairly sure that whoever was there hadn't noticed me arrive.

Relieved, I peered around the side of the slide to see what was happening, but it was too dark to make much out. My heart was beating hard and my hands shook. Somehow, I managed to remember that my compu-wristband had a setting for night vision to help me see in the dark. I flicked it on and slowly everything started to become clearer.

The life forms I could see in front of me looked like Fayans, but I knew immediately that they weren't. I realised from their strange clothes and the fur on top of their heads that they were the local inhabitants of K22 that we had heard about.

They were standing next to some hover-scooters that had been parked close by, and they looked puzzled, as though they had no idea what the scooters were.

After a moment, two of the locals picked up a scooter. I crept forward, and saw them carry it to an odd-looking square metal box with wheels on it that was sitting nearby. I realised that the box was a transport vehicle of some kind. Fayans had vehicles like that hundreds of years ago. I had seen them in museums. I watched as the locals lifted the scooter together and loaded it into the tray at the back of the vehicle. Then they climbed into the front and sped off.

I needed to know what was going on. Why had they taken a scooter? Without thinking, I rushed over, grabbed another scooter, and took off after the vehicle. Hover-scooters use air to propel them along and are completely silent, so I knew I wouldn't be heard. And, because I had my night vision on, I didn't need lights, so I wouldn't be seen either.

I rode behind the vehicle for some time. We passed through empty city streets and then along a big, wide, empty road. Finally, we left the city and travelled into a strange, open expanse, with a few houses and half-dead trees in the distance.

Checking my position on the map on my compu-wristband, I realised I had travelled a long way from the ship. It suddenly occurred to me that I should tell someone where I was. I tried to contact my guardians, but the calls failed to connect.

I was starting to panic slightly when the face of my compu-wristband began to glow with an incoming call. It was Komot.

Chapter 4
Outside the City

"Where are you?" Komot demanded.

"Where are *you*?" I replied.

"It's all right, I can see you now," she said.

There was a whoosh of air and suddenly Komot was right next to me. I almost jumped out of my scooter seat.

"What are you doing here?" I hissed.

"Nice to see you, too," she replied, laughing. "I couldn't sleep and heard some strange rumbling outside. I put my night vision on and I saw you taking off on your scooter. So I tracked you, but it's taken me all this time to catch up."

I quickly filled her in on what I had seen, and told her about how I couldn't contact the ship.

"I had the same problem. There must be something blocking the communication," she said, frowning.

"I suppose we'll just have to follow these life forms, then," I said. "And when we find out where they are, we can mark it on our compu-maps and head back to the ship to let them know."

After a few minutes, the vehicle turned off the main road, towards a small settlement. Soon it slowed down and drove through a gateway. Komot and I rode up to the gateway and peered in. The vehicle had stopped and the engine was off. The four locals were getting out.

I signalled to Komot to ride up the street a little. We left our scooters and crept around the back of a building, near where the vehicle was parked.

We watched as the locals unloaded the scooter and carried it to an open shed.

"I'm going to try and get a bit closer," I whispered to Komot.

"No!" she said, grabbing at my arm.

"I'll be fine," I responded, scurrying forward. "I just need to see what they are doing."

One of the locals touched part of the wall and suddenly the shed was flooded with light. I could see them all.

Unfortunately, they could see me, too.

Chapter 5
Caught

My first thought was to turn back. But that would lead them to Komot. Instead, I tried to run around the side of the building to avoid the light.

But, after being asleep for ten years, my body wasn't quite ready to move quickly again. My feet felt like lead. In seconds, the four locals had caught up with me and were pulling me back towards the shed. Each of them was yelling, and the sound of their voices was squeaky and irritating. I had no idea what they were saying.

Suddenly, one of them pointed to my hands, and for a moment they were all silent. I looked down at my three fingers and then looked at their hands with five fingers each.

"I'm from planet Faya," I said.

One of them pulled back a little, as though I was speaking too loudly.

"I am Okadi," I said, pointing to myself.

But they just stared at me as though I was some kind of monster.

Just then, Komot's voice came to me through my compu-wristband. She said she was back on her scooter and was going to get help. The group could hear her, too, but because we couldn't understand each other's languages, I was sure they had no idea what she was saying. However, the sounds made the locals curious. They gathered around me and prodded at the wristband.

They didn't seem unfriendly, but then it was hard to know. If only I could speak to them. Then I remembered I had downloaded the folders with the pictures and writing in their language. There was an image in there that I knew I could use to help me communicate. I tried to touch my wristband, but they stopped me and instead attempted to pull it off, which made me cry out.

"Let go!" I shouted.

The force of my voice did something strange to them. They all staggered backwards, clutching their heads.

I thought about how quiet their voices sounded to me, and I suddenly realised that my voice must sound loud to them. My shout must have felt like a thunderclap.

While the locals recovered from the shout, I had a moment to access my compu-wristband. I quickly found the files and beamed them onto the shed wall.

The group gazed at them, stunned, as I flicked from one image to another. Finally, I found the one that I wanted. It looked to me like a picture of the solar system we were in. I turned to them, careful to speak softly, so as not to deafen anyone.

"Is this you?" I asked quietly, pointing to the third planet from the sun.

They stared at me suspiciously.

I pointed to myself, then I pointed back to the picture, but to a spot further out, past the last planet in their solar system.

"Okadi," I said. "I come from across the universe."

One of them walked up to me and cautiously touched my hand. It was so strange to see these people up close. Despite the differences, we were really quite similar. We held each other's eyes for a moment.

One of the group pointed to themselves and said something that sounded like "Nat."

I repeated it, trying to make the same sounds. The local nodded and smiled, so I guessed that Nat was his name and I had pronounced it correctly.

One of the others pointed to herself and said, "Jo." Then she indicated the two others and said, "Bill. Kira."

Jo picked up a stick and started drawing markings on the ground. She drew a picture of our spaceship and pointed to me. I nodded. The four of them then spoke among themselves for a while, occasionally glancing over in my direction.

While they were talking, I looked around. The sun had started to rise and I could see things around me a little better. There were several sheds and some large water tanks. Not far away was a stand of trees. These ones were alive. While they didn't look exactly like the trees from hundreds of years ago that I had seen pictures of on Faya, they were close enough for me to recognise. I couldn't believe how beautiful they were.

Chapter 6

We Need a Translation

Just then, my compu-wristband lit up and Komot's voice crackled through the speaker. "We're almost there!" she said.

Bill, Jo, Kira and Nat moved towards me and stared at my compu-wristband. They all started to talk very loudly … well, loudly for them, at least. Then, I saw Nat look up and past me. He let out a gasp.

I turned to see what he was looking at, and there, behind us, was a squad of Fayans on their scooters, with Olag, my guardian, at the front.

Olag looked alarmed. “Release Okadi!” he shouted.

I was fairly sure that the four locals could not understand what Olag was saying. But they certainly felt the force of his voice, which seemed to hit them like a blast, pushing them backwards and forcing them to block their ears with their fingers.

Olag stared at them, “What’s happening?” he asked.

“Shh!” I said. “I think it’s our voices. We sound extremely loud to them. A shout can hurt them.”

“But they can’t understand us?”

“No,” I replied.

Just then, Komot stepped forward.

“We can fix that,” she said. “Remember those strange folders you scanned and uploaded into your compu-wristband? That went into the super-compu last night, and it has worked out a translation program. It’s being installed into our wristbands right now.”

Olag spoke quietly into the translation program on his compu-wristband. He said, “We are from planet Faya and we come in peace.”

The four locals looked up as they heard familiar words coming from the wristband's speaker as it translated the message. They looked puzzled and repeated the same words back to us.

This in turn was translated back to Fayan as, "We are a planet of farmers and we welcome the quiet."

"That program might need a bit of work," I said, trying not to laugh.

Olag nodded, but we both knew it was a start. At least the locals seemed open to talking to us.

Chapter 7

Our Planet or Your Planet?

Over the rest of the day, we improved the translation program and got to know Nat, Jo, Kira and Bill better. They invited us to eat with them. Kira told us that they had grown the food themselves.

They told us that they call their planet "Earth", which is also a name for the soil under our feet. They called themselves "humans". They belonged to one of the groups who had survived after a series of natural disasters overwhelmed the planet many years before, wiping out much of the population. Those who were left created settlements around patches of land that could be farmed. They said there were many groups like them around the countryside.

They had seen us land the spaceship the day before, and crept into the city after dark to find out who we were. They said they had taken one of the hover-scooters because they wanted to investigate our technology.

The meal was almost over when we noticed a glint of light high up in the sky.

"What's that?" Kira asked. I could hear fear in her voice.

The humans got up and stared as a shiny form came into view in the distance.

"It's one of our spaceships," said Komot.

"Another one!" said Nat. "How many are there?"

I looked to Olag, but his compu-wristband had lit up and he stepped away from the group to talk to someone.

"There are only three other spaceships," I said. "The population of our planet was not very big in the end."

"But still," said Nat. "There will be thousands of you once they all arrive. You're going to take over."

"We had no choice in coming here. This was the only place we could live. We hope you will help us," I said.

Just then, Olag announced that we needed to return to the ship. When I turned back to the humans again, they were walking away. I called out goodbye, but they didn't look back.

Chapter 8

Rebuilding Together

When we arrived back in the city, the other spaceship had landed. It felt like a party, with Fayans everywhere, laughing and greeting each other. The new arrivals told us that the other two ships would come in the next day or so.

A community meeting was called and the pilot of the second ship told us they had circled the planet several times, scanning for life.

"Some parts of the planet have been badly affected by the environmental disasters, but a lot of the plant and animal life seems to be returning. The human settlements, although small and far apart, are surviving, but they have lost a lot of their technology and ways of communicating," he said.

Then our pilot stepped up. “The space probes from years ago indicated that most of K22 was occupied. We made plans to live in desert areas which were uninhabited and could be transformed with our technology into fertile land. The conditions here have changed, and we will have to rethink everything. I believe now that our first step is to help the surviving humans rebuild their planet,” she said.

The crowd cheered in agreement.

The next day, Komot and I took our hover-scooters and rode back out to where we had met Bill, Kira, Jo and Nat. We looked around the sheds, but they were nowhere to be seen. I was afraid they had left to escape us. We were about to return to the spaceship when I noticed some movement in the trees nearby.

"Please talk to us," I said into my compu-wristband translation program.

"We only want to help," added Komot.

After a few moments, the four humans emerged from the trees and walked towards us.

"Why should we trust you?" asked Jo.

"Look at this," I said.

I found a flat rock nearby and projected some files from my compu-wristband.

"These are pictures of where we came from," I said. "As our sun grew hotter, it dried out our planet and slowly killed life. Fayans had to work hard to look after what little we had. We learnt to use less water, to recycle and reuse everything. We also had to respect each other and work together cooperatively to survive."

"And we promise to help you to do the same here on Earth," added Komot.

Over the months that followed, we contacted human groups all around the planet. While we wanted to make Earth our home, we also wanted to help the humans. We were going to be living together, after all. We began by fixing satellite communications, and worked on repairing and restoring technology.

In turn, the humans taught us about their beautiful planet and the plants and animals that live here. They showed us how to grow food and build with local materials. Now, our two groups are learning each other's languages and slowly becoming friends.

The only thing we Fayans have to remember is to always speak quietly!